The Fox with Cold Feet

by Bill Singer

pictures by
Dennis Kendrick

Parents Magazine Press • New York

for Joan, Mark, and Eric—B.S.

to Dad and Lib—D.K.

10   9   8   7   6   5   4   3   2   1

Library of Congress Cataloging in Publication Data
Singer, Bill.   The fox with cold feet.
SUMMARY: Wanting to protect his feet from the snow,
Fox collects an odd assortment of make-shift boots from
his animal friends for doing them favors, but
just who benefits more is questionable.
[1. Shoes and boots—Fiction.   2. Foxes—Fiction.
3. Animals—Fiction]   I. Kendrick, Dennis.   II. Title.
PZ7.S6157Fo   [E]   80–10288
ISBN 0–8193–1021–2   ISBN 0–8193–1022–0 lib. bdg.

One crisp morning young Fox
leaped out of his den.
A thick blanket of snow
covered the ground.

Just then, Sparrow flew by, looking for seeds.

Fox was pleased with himself.
He sang an old fox song:

Fox followed Sparrow to the
bare elm tree where she lived.

She tugged at an empty nest,
and it fell to the ground.

CRUNCH!   CRUNCH!

Fox tried to run,
but he couldn't.
So he slowly made his way
uphill and downhill until
he came to a frozen pond.
Beaver was adding branches
to his dam.

So young Fox carried
branch after branch.
He kept looking
for a boot under the wood.
But he didn't see one.
Finally, he brought the last
branch to Beaver.

Here's your boot.

I'm quick and spry,
clever and sly.

But it seemed better than nothing.
And Fox went off to see if Raccoon could help him.

Fox slipped and slid through the snow.
At last he came to a hollow tree.

Soon Raccoon peeked
out of the hollow tree.

Raccoon slowly stepped out of the hollow tree
and dragged himself through the forest.

Fox followed, slipping and sliding in the snow.
At last they came to an old campsite.

So Fox pushed...

and pulled...

and pushed.

At last the garbage can fell over.
Then he pulled the lid off.

Of course. Here's one.

Take your time.
Get used to your new boots.

CRUNCH! CLUNK! THUD! THUNK!

THUD! THUNK!

PLOP!

Aha! I know what to do.

THUNK!

PLOP!

Fox ran all the way back
to his den, never
tripping, slipping, sliding, or falling.

And at last
Fox was right.